D1624021

cuc 10
1/14

DUE DATE

THE CHICAGO PUBLIC LIBRARY

AUSTIN-IRVING BRANCH
6100 WEST IRVING PARK
CHICAGO, IL 60634

Winona's Pony Cart

The Betsy-Tacy books:

The Deep Valley books:

Winona's Pony Cart

Maud Hart Lovelace

Illustrated by Vera Neville

HarperCollins*Publishers*

LC Number 53-8417
First Harper Trophy edition, 2000

Visit us on the World Wide Web!
www.harperchildrens.com

For
STEPHEN *and* CATHY BOND,
BONNIE CROWE,
and
LEA *and* ANN AVERY

Contents

Winona's Pony Cart

1

Winona and Toodles

WINONA ROOT and her pug dog Toodles were sitting on the wall which hemmed in one side of the large Root lawn. Winona was cross.

"Dignified! Dignified!" she was saying crossly. She kicked her heels against the white stones of the wall. It hurt, but she didn't care.

She was saying "dignified" because her mother had told her that she ought to be more so.

Her mother had come out of doors a little while before to call Winona in, and had found her sitting on top of the bird bath. This marble bowl stood on a tall pedestal out on the front lawn. Winona had been calling, "Giddap! Giddap!" and bouncing up and down and slapping imaginary reins. She was pretending, of course, to be riding a pony.

Naturally, she had gotten wet—her dress, her two petticoats, even her panties. There was water in a bird bath; wasn't there? Was *that* her fault? If she had a pony she wouldn't have to go riding on so many other things.

But her mother hadn't waited to hear these explanations. She had been much annoyed, perhaps because she was entertaining the Ladies' Foreign Missionary Society, and Winona was wearing her very best dress. She had been supposed to pass the candy around.

"Well," her mother had said slowly, "you can't pass candy now."

"But I *want* to pass it!" Winona had wailed.

"And you can't have any refreshments."

"But I *want* some refreshments!" Winona had scrambled down from the bird bath, dripping and crying.

Her mother had paid no attention. She spoke gently, as she always did, but her voice was as firm as a rock. "Go in the back door and up the back stairs. Change your clothes, and then take Toodles and sit out on the wall until my guests go home."

She picked up the skirt of her gray silk dress and started to go away. But she stopped and gave Winona a look. It was a sort of sad, discouraged look as though she was thinking, what on earth am I going to do with this child!

"Winona," she said, "you're almost eight years old. You ought to be more dignified."

"Dignified!" Winona said now, as she sat on the wall with Toodles.

Toodles was asleep. Winona knew he was asleep because his tail was uncurled. When Toodles was awake his tail curled up as tight as a doughnut on his smooth yellow hip. But when he was asleep it hung as straight as a sausage.

Winona kept on kicking the wall. "This house is too dignified whatsoever," she said.

The house stood on a corner, catercorner to the school house. It was dignified, all right. It was a large brick house, painted white, with dark green shutters and porches on every side. The lawn was full of trees: tall oaks and elms and maples. The leaves were turning red and yellow and orange and brown and pink.

"Getting ready for your birthday," her father had told her at dinner. The trees were always brightly colored for Winona's birthday because it came in October.

On the side nearest the school, the lawn followed Pleasant Street down a steep hill. It was hemmed in by that wall on which Winona was sitting. On the other side it ran flat along School Street and ended in a hedge. The bird bath stood here with flower beds on either side.

From this upper lawn a terrace rolled down to the lower lawn, which Winona especially liked. There was a swing down there, and room for the croquet set. Best of all, there was lots and lots of grassy space to play in. On the alley was the small corral where Ole, the hired man, exercised her father's bangtailed riding horse, Bob, and her mother's carriage horse, Florence. The carriage house stood near, and the barn where Bob and Florence lived.

There was an empty stall in the barn, just the right size for that pony Winona wished she had. And Ole had plenty of time to take care of a pony.

"He wouldn't mind at all," Winona thought. Old Ole liked horses better than people. He told her so often, especially when he found her climbing on Bob or Florence, or playing with the harness in his tidy harness closet, or pretending to ride in her mother's carriage—an elegant surrey with a brown fringed top.

All of a sudden Winona had a wonderful idea.

"I might," she thought, "ask for a pony for my birthday."

Of course, she had already asked for a little printing press, and her father had said he couldn't afford it. And she had asked for a doll as big as a baby, jointed, with yellow hair and eyes that opened and shut, and he had said he couldn't afford that. But he always said he couldn't afford the things she asked for. He would say he didn't have any money, and then he would laugh and jingle some in his pocket. And, oftener than not, she got what she wanted.

"He spoils me. Everyone says so," Winona thought hopefully.

Maybe she'd ask him tonight! Or maybe she shouldn't, because it would remind her mother of how she had gone riding on the bird bath? Her mother hadn't liked that a bit.

"My mother is too *dignified*," Winona thought, kicking the wall hard with her black high-buttoned shoes.

Her mother was very dignified. She was president

of the Ladies' Foreign Missionary Society. She was slender and frail and always beautifully dressed, with never a hair out of place.

Winona's sisters were dignified, too. Of course, they were young ladies. Bessie was fifteen and Myra was thirteen; they wore shirt waists and skirts and pompadours. They liked to study and to do embroidery, and Bessie painted place cards and fans and copied Gibson Girl heads. Myra was planning to marry a minister. Not any special minister; she just liked ministers.

Winona wasn't a bit like either of them.

Winona had black eyes that snapped and flashed with mischief. Her face was tanned, and a mane of black hair was always flying out behind her. She liked to be outdoors, to play wild games, and run, and climb trees.

"This is my *western* daughter," Winona's mother always said when introducing Winona. She would explain with a loving smile that the two older girls had been born back in New York state while Winona had been born here in Deep Valley, Minnesota.

"She means I'm a tomboy," Winona thought bitterly and kicked the wall so hard that she yelled, "Ouch!" and Toodles woke up.

He looked at her with his bulging dark eyes.

He had a comical little black face full of worried-looking wrinkles.

"Prob'ly he worries about me," Winona thought. "Toodles," she said, putting her face down on his soft yellow back, "I'm the only one in this whole family that isn't dignified. Even Father is, a little."

Her father was a tall, important-looking man. Across his starched white vest he wore a heavy gold watch chain with a Knights of Pythias fob. He had black hair and eyes like Winona's, and white teeth like hers, and perhaps when he was a little boy he hadn't been dignified either. Certainly he always understood what made her do the things she did. He always helped her out when she got into fixes.

"He isn't *very* dignified," Winona said. "Not any more than he has to be, when he's editor of the paper."

He was publisher and editor of the *Deep Valley Sun*. Winona liked to go down to his office and watch the busy presses. Not long ago he had bought a self-setting type machine. A linotype machine, it was called. He said it was a wonderful new invention. He had shown it to her and explained it to her just as though she were grown up. He had let her sit on the operator's lap and push the keys and spell out her name in type.

It was on account of this that Winona had asked

for that printing press for her birthday.

In September, when school began, he let her walk around the printing shop and pick out whatever she wanted—ink and pencil tablets, and clean note pads, and a full new box of pencils sharpened to fine points. He had her name printed on her notebooks. Betsy Ray, a girl in Winona's class at school, always envied her that.

"I'd like *my* name printed on a notebook. I'd write a book in it," she said.

Winona's father was having the invitations to her birthday party printed at the paper. He was going to bring them home tonight.

Winona remembered how nice her father was.

"Yes, I *will* ask for a pony," she decided. "But perhaps I'd better go in and practice my music lesson."

Her father often asked her at supper whether she had practiced. He was anxious for her to learn to play the piano. She was supposed to practice half an hour twice a day. But she didn't always do it. There was too much to do out of doors.

"But, Winona, you like music, just as I do. You'd be good at it," he would say. "After you learn to play, you can play for me in the evening."

"Yes, I'd better go in and practice," Winona thought, jumping up. But then she remembered the

Ladies' Foreign Missionary Society, and she sat down again.

"I can't practice," she thought with satisfaction. "And it isn't my fault. Prob'ly they'll stay so late I can't practice at all. Too bad! I might get so I could play beautiful pieces for Father. I might get to be a famous piano player, if it wasn't for that old Foreign Missionary Society . . . in there eating up the refreshments."

Toodles growled sympathetically, but after a minute he fell asleep again. And Winona grew crosser and crosser. It was lonesome, sitting on the wall.

2

Winona and Her Friends

SOME SYRIAN children came toiling up the hill. They were coming from the Catholic school on the north end of town and going to their homes on the south end of town in a valley called Little Syria.

Winona liked the Syrians. They were dark and foreign-looking and talked in an exciting way, waving their hands. They loved bright colors, and she did, too. Her father had asked her mother please to let Winona wear bright colors because she loved them so. Her mother favored dark blue sailor suits, with white dresses for Sunday.

The Syrian girls wore gay-colored head scarfs, and red ribbons woven into their braids. They wore earrings and glass bracelets, and the boys put feathers in their caps and flowers in their buttonholes.

They had come to know Winona, passing her house so much. Sometimes they stopped and turned her jump rope. Sometimes they joined her in hop scotch on the walk. A boy named Scundar often threw her a ball as he passed, and Winona would throw it back to him, and he would throw it back to her. A little girl named Marium often stopped to pet Toodles.

She stopped to pet Toodles now, and Scundar asked, "Would you like to toss the ball?"

But Winona had to shake her head.

The Syrian children went on.

Winona looked dismally across at the school house, a red brick building trimmed with yellow stone. There was a flight of steep stone steps leading to the big front door. Whenever it was time for school to begin, a boy stood on those steps and rang a bell. Winona lived so near that she didn't

need to start to school until she heard that bell—
unless she wanted to. Sometimes she ran over early
for the fun of playing in the girls' yard.

School was over now. The girls' yard and the
boys' yard were empty. But after a while Winona
saw a boy named Dennie come running down the
school house steps.

He had been kept late because he had brought a
garter snake to school and put it in a box of erasers.
Miss Canning, the teacher, hadn't liked it.

"What did she do to you?" Winona called as he
came near.

"Aw, she just scolded me!" Dennie tossed his
curly head. He stopped beside the wall. Dennie
liked Winona. He had once left a stick of gum on
her desk.

"I'll race you down the hill," he said.

Winona wished she could do it, but she had to
say no. She had to sit on the wall.

Lottie and Lettie Pepper came up the hill next,
pulling an empty cart. They had come to fetch the
laundry. Their mother did the washing for the
Roots. Lottie and Lettie were twins and looked just
alike, thin and wiry, with bright blue, interested
eyes.

"Want to do tricks?" they asked.

They often stayed to do tricks when they came to

get the laundry or to bring it back. They could stand on each other's shoulders, and were teaching Winona to do it.

"Yes, I *want* to, but that doesn't mean I can," Winona answered.

Lottie and Lettie took their cart around to the back door and received a brimming laundry basket from Selma, the Roots' hired girl. They pulled the cart back down the hill and disappeared.

For a while there were only horses going up and down the hill, pulling surreys and buggies and delivery wagons. A load of hay went past, and Winona wished on it; she wished for a pony.

The street-sprinkling cart went past. That was fun, as a rule. It sprinkled water as it moved along the street, and you could run out and play in it and get wet. She couldn't today.

The rag man went past in his mysterious wagon. He was calling, "Rags! Rags! Any rags today?" If she hadn't had to sit on the wall, Winona could have followed him down the street. She might have seen him weigh somebody's bundle of old clothes and give them a shiny pan or muffin tin in return.

"Double darn!" Winona said, although she knew it was practically swearing.

Three little girls came out of Mrs. Chubbock's candy store, next door to the school house. They were in Miss Canning's room too. Their names were Betsy, Tacy, and Tib.

Betsy Ray, the one who liked Winona's notebooks, had a round face with short braids sticking out behind. Her front teeth were parted in the middle. Tacy Kelly had long red ringlets and Tib Muller was little and cute with yellow curls.

"Want to play?" they called now, running across the street.

This was too much, Winona thought! Everyone could play except her! The Syrian children, and Dennie, and Lottie and Lettie.

"If I did, I'd have plenty of people to play with," she answered, scowling.

That made them mad.

"You think you're pretty important," said Betsy, "just because your father runs the newspaper. Well, my father is so handsome that people stop him on the street to tell him how handsome he is! Just last night old Mrs. Murphy stopped him right in front of his shoe store. She said he got handsomer every day."

"He gives her shoes for nothing," Tib explained. Winona saw Betsy and Tacy poke her to keep still.

"My father can play the violin," said Tacy quickly. "He's as good as Ole Bull, just about."

Tib thought only a moment. "My father can eat

spoiled catsup," she said. "He did it once and it didn't make him sick."

The three of them looked at Winona defiantly.

"Who's talking about fathers?" asked Winona. "I'll bet you can't guess who kissed me once?"

Betsy, Tacy, and Tib burst into scornful laughter.

"We don't like kissing talk!"

"We hate it!"

"We don't like boys!"

"Joke on you!" said Winona. "It wasn't any old boy. I'll tell you who it was because you never could guess. It was Buffalo Bill!"

"Buffalo Bill!" They were astounded.

Winona nodded importantly. "Yup!" she said. "Buffalo Bill kissed me."

He had, too.

It was over a year ago when she was only six. He had been in town with his Wild West Show, and after the parade down Main Street, he had brought his band to serenade the office of the *Deep Valley Sun*. Winona had been hoisted up into the glittery wagon. Buffalo Bill, with his broad-brimmed black hat, his piercing eyes, his mustaches and spike of beard, had held her by the hand.

The band had played, and the music had sounded frighteningly loud, and the bandmen in their gaudy uniforms had looked frighteningly strange. Buffalo

Bill had stood straight as an Indian holding Winona's hand, and at the end he had picked her up and kissed her.

Winona had been terribly afraid. She knew better than to cry with her father and a whole crowd of people looking on. She hadn't liked it, though.

"I didn't like it," she said now to Betsy, Tacy, and Tib. "His mustaches tickled."

That made them laugh.

"Want a jelly bean?" asked Betsy, holding out the bag.

"Yup!" Winona answered, and Betsy, Tacy, and Tib hopped up on the wall beside her.

It was nice sitting there in the late afternoon sunshine. Red and yellow leaves drifted down upon their heads.

"You have a lot of leaves on this big lawn," said Betsy. "Do you ever play in them?"

"I should say I do," Winona answered. She munched a jelly bean and gave one to Toodles. He wasn't supposed to have them, but she didn't care today. "My father doesn't burn up the leaves until after my birthday," she said. "He leaves them just on purpose so I can play in them."

"What do you play?" Tacy asked.

"I rake them into a house. You know—parlor and dining room and kitchen and bedrooms with piles of leaves for walls."

"I'd be good at that," said Tib, "because my father is an architect. I could tell you where to put in closets and halls and things."

"Betsy could make up a story about us all living in that leaf house," said Tacy.

"Could you?" asked Winona.

"Of course," said Betsy. "We could have a big fight with the people next door."

"A terrible fight! We'd get so mad we'd all throw leaves," said Tacy, and her eyes began to sparkle.

"We'd throw so many leaves it would be the end of the house!"

"Why don't we do it now?" asked Tib. "We can stay a little while."

Winona wriggled uncomfortably. "Maybe your mothers wouldn't want you to stay," she suggested.

"Oh, they wouldn't mind!" Betsy replied.

"Betsy and I were playing over at Tib's house," Tacy explained. "We found a nickel down a crack in the sidewalk, and Tib's mother let us come and buy candy."

"She wouldn't worry if we were a little slow coming back," added Tib. "Where do you keep your rake?"

But Winona had to shake her head.

"Toodles and I have to sit here on this wall," she

said hastily. "We're . . . we're waiting for something. I can't tell you what it is, but it's something awfully dignified!"

"What does 'dignified' mean?" asked Tib.

"Important," said Betsy. "Oh, well! We'll come and make the leaf house some other day."

"When is your birthday?" asked Tib. "Are you having a party?"

"A week from today. Of course, I'm having a party."

"Ice cream?" asked Betsy.

"Of course."

"Birthday cake?" asked Tacy.

"Of course!"

Everyone looked interested.

"What do you want for your birthday?" Tib inquired.

"A pony!" said Winona. It was wonderful to say it. Saying it right out loud like that sort of made up for having to sit on the wall.

"A pony!" cried Tib. "Why, I don't know anyone that's got a pony!" Betsy and Tacy nudged her to keep still.

"Oh, a pony isn't so much!" said Betsy. "Maybe *you'll* get one for *your* birthday, Tib. I'll bet you will. Don't you bet so, Tacy?"

"I'm practically sure of it," said Tacy.

"Oh, my papa couldn't afford one!" answered Tib. Betsy and Tacy nudged her again.

"Maybe Tacy will get one," said Betsy. "Her father has a horse, and so has mine."

"Would you like a pony, Betsy?" Tacy asked in a careless voice.

"Well, sort of! I wouldn't mind!"

"I'll bet you wouldn't mind!" Winona jeered.

The front door of her house opened and the ladies of the Foreign Missionary Society began to come out. They were wearing hats and jackets, or short capes, and they caught up their sweeping skirts in their hands as they started down the porch steps. They were telling Winona's mother that it had been a splendid meeting and the refreshments were delicious.

Several of them got into a surrey that had driven up in front. And others got into a phaeton that Ole brought around from the driveway. The rest started off down the walk, still holding their skirts daintily off the ground.

When everyone was out of sight, Mrs. Root came to the door.

"Winona!" she called. "You may come in now and practice your music lesson."

Betsy, Tacy, and Tib whirled upon Winona.

"Winona Root!" cried Betsy. "You were just sitting here because you had to!"

"You were being punished!" cried Tacy.

"But you said it was something dignified!" cried Tib, bewildered.

"Yes," said Betsy crushingly. "She said she was going to get a pony, too."

"Winona!" called Mrs. Root again. "You *must* come in and practice. It's almost time for supper."

Toodles heard the word "supper" and struggled to his feet. Toodles loved to eat. That was why he was so fat. He curled his tail and started up the walk, but he stopped and waited for Winona.

Winona was dancing a jig on the wall. This was to show that she didn't care because they had found her out.

Betsy, Tacy, and Tib started to go home.

"Can we come over and rake?" asked Tib.

"Sure," said Winona teasingly. "But come before my birthday. After that, I'll be busy with my pony."

"Pony!" cried Betsy in exasperation.

"Pony! Pony!" cried Tacy and Tib.

"Pony!" they all cried together.

"P-O-N-" began Winona but she stopped. She wasn't sure whether she should say "Y" or "I-E." Winona wasn't very good at spelling.

"Winona!" called her mother sternly and started down the steps.

"I'm coming," shouted Winona. "Ta ta," she said over her shoulder to Betsy, Tacy, and Tib.

"Ta ta," they answered, waving.

Winona was laughing but inside she felt determined.

"I have to, I just have to get a pony for my birthday," she thought as she hurried up the walk.

3
Party Invitations

THAT EVENING Winona's mother addressed the party invitations. Mr. Root had brought them home at supper time, elegantly printed on gold-edged pink cards. There were fifteen of them.

"For fifteen children! And Winona makes sixteen. Two children at the party for every year of her life," Mrs. Root said, smiling. She was happy about the invitations. She hadn't even mentioned Winona going riding on the bird bath. Maybe she had forgotten about it, Winona thought. She hoped so, on account of the pony.

Mrs. Root looked nice in her gray silk dress. The yoke and high boned collar were of gray lace over pink. Some of the pinkness seemed to have crept up into her soft pale cheeks. The skirt swirled out around her slender figure as she sat writing at the library desk.

This was really Mr. Root's desk, and the library was really his room, but the family liked it. They often sat here in the evening.

There was a fire in the fireplace tonight. Toodles was stretched out in front of the dancing flames. Toodles loved the fire. You couldn't persuade him to go for a walk after a fire had been lighted. He would cough or wheeze and pretend that he had a cold. Now he was sleeping, with his tongue hanging out—his tail uncurled, of course.

The library had tall shelves full of books. There was a red plush lounge with a bolster, and above it hung a gold-framed oil painting that Winona particularly liked. An artist had painted it down at her father's office. It showed a table and upon it were a copy of the *Deep Valley Sun*, a half-smoked cigar, a violin and a mouse.

What, Winona always wondered, was a mouse doing there? And the violin was almost as mysterious. Her father couldn't even play the violin. But the newspaper looked as though he had just put it down, and she could fairly smell that cigar.

He was smoking one now as he sat reading in his big leather chair.

Bessie and Myra were doing their homework beside the center table which had a gas lamp with a green glass shade. It was good to study by. There was a basket chair where Mrs. Root liked to sit and crochet, but tonight she was sitting in front of the desk.

She sat very straight, as she always did. Mrs. Root was sick a good deal, but she never acted sick. She never complained and always tried to do whatever she was supposed to.

"Win," Winona's father had said to her one day, "I know your mother expects you children to be perfect. And it's hard on you sometimes. But don't forget, Win, that first of all she tries to be perfect herself."

Winona leaned on her mother's chair and watched her address the party invitations.

One went to a little girl named Joyce. She and Winona had started to be friends because she came from a town named Winona, and Winona's name was Winona, and they thought that was a joke. She was a fat, jolly girl with a fat braid of butter-colored hair.

Another invitation went to a boy named Percy. Mrs. Root liked him better than Winona did. Winona thought he was a sissy because he wore ruffled blouses. And he had curls—not merry, tousled curls like Dennie's but neat, blond curls that used to be long. His father had insisted on cutting them, Mrs. Root had remarked one night at supper.

"Hooray for him!" Mr. Root had answered. Mr. Root liked Percy's father. They went riding together.

"Do we have to have Percy?" Winona asked as her mother addressed his invitation in her graceful, precise handwriting.

"Certainly," her mother replied. "He's one of your best friends."

Invitations went to every child in Winona's Sunday School class, and the rest went mostly to children whose mothers were friends of Winona's mother. Just as Mrs. Root finished the last invitation it dawned on Winona that there were lots more children she'd like to have invited.

"Mother," she said, "I'd like to ask Dennie."

"Dennie?" said her mother. "I don't believe I know him."

"He stopped to talk to me just this afternoon when I was sitting on the wall," Winona said. "He had been kept after school."

"Why?" asked her mother. "What for?"

"Oh . . . nothing much!" Winona was sorry she had mentioned it. "He just put something into a basket of erasers."

"What was it?" her mother persisted.

"Oh . . . just a garter snake."

"A garter snake!" Her mother jumped as though one had run up her silken skirt. Bessie and Myra squealed delightedly, and Mr. Root laughed out loud.

"It was a very little one," Winona cried. "And garter snakes can't hurt you. You know that; don't you, Mother?"

"Never mind!" said her mother. "All our invitations are used up. See? Father had fifteen printed and we've addressed them all, so we couldn't possibly invite anyone else."

"Oh, dear!" Winona cried, for the more she thought about her party, the more she thought of people she would like to invite—the Syrian children, and Lottie and Lettie, and Betsy, Tacy, and Tib.

"Couldn't Father . . ." she began, but her mother stood up. She shook the invitations into a neat pack between her slender fingers.

"Just fifteen," she said firmly, smiling. "And every one is written. It's bedtime, Winona."

"Oh, dear!" Winona said again.

She kissed her mother, and she kissed Bessie and Myra. When she reached her father, she climbed into his lap. She put her black head on his shoulder, and he gave her a hug. It seemed like a good time to ask for a pony.

"Father," she said, "I practiced my music lesson after school today."

"Did you, Win?" he asked. He often called her Win because it was a boy's name and he said she was the only boy he had.

"I practiced awfully good," Winona said. "I think I can play pieces pretty soon. I'll play them for you in the evening."

"That will be nice," he answered.

Winona snuggled down cozily. "Father, do you know what I want for my birthday?"

"Of course. You told me."

"What?"

"A printing press, and a doll as big as a baby."

"And a pony," said Winona dreamily.

"A pony!" He spoke loudly in surprise. Mrs. Root, who had gone to her basket chair and picked up her crocheting, looked up quickly. Winona thought perhaps she had better tell her father what had happened that afternoon.

"I really need a pony," she said, speaking fast. "I have to go pony-riding on the bird bath, and I get all wet, and it's a wonder I don't break it."

"It certainly is," he cut in.

"But that's the only pony I've got," said Winona. "The only pony whatsoever."

Mrs. Root put down her crocheting. She looked at her husband earnestly.

"Horace," she said. "About that bird bath incident! It made me see more clearly than ever that Winona must be trained to be more ladylike."

"See here!" said Mr. Root, and he patted Winona's hair. "Win is the only boy I've got."

"But she isn't a boy. She's a girl and will soon be a young lady. And I want her to be quiet and gentle and modest like her sisters . . ."

Bessie and Myra looked up at Winona and smiled. Myra almost winked, but of course she didn't. She was going to marry a minister.

Her sisters liked Winona just as she was. She was so much younger that they made a pet of her. Bessie had made her a set of hand-painted paper dolls. And Myra curled Winona's hair for Sundays and parties; she put it up on rags.

They were smiling at her fondly, but Mrs. Root wasn't smiling.

"A pony," she said, "would only encourage Winona in her tomboy ways."

"Hear that, Win?" her father asked, and Winona knew what he meant. About some things he always minded Mother. He said Mother knew more than he did about raising girls.

Winona slipped off his lap and looked up at that picture she liked. She looked hard at the mouse. What *was* it doing there? She was trying not to cry.

"I'm afraid you'll have to be satisfied with Toodles," her father said. He sounded sorry.

Toodles heard his name and got to his feet, stretching and curling his tail. He always went to bed with Winona. He was supposed to sleep in his basket, in a corner of the library. It was a comfortable boat-shaped basket with a red and brown blanket inside. But he went upstairs when Winona did and curled up on the foot of her bed.

When Mr. and Mrs. Root went to bed they called him down and put him in his basket. It didn't do any good. As soon as the door of their room was closed, he sneaked back to Winona.

He ran upstairs ahead of her now, as fast as his short legs would take him. At the top he paused and

barked for her to hurry. Winona followed glumly.

She liked her room. It had fluffy yellow curtains, and the yellowish-brown matting on the floor smelled pleasant, like hay. All her toys and books were here. Her doll house stood in a corner.

Selma had lighted the gas jet and turned it down low.

Winona went to the east window. There were two windows in her room. One looked north down Pleasant Street Hill. The east one looked over the roof of the back porch to the barn where Bob and Florence were sleeping. She wondered whether they were standing up or lying down. Horses could sleep standing up; Ole had told her so.

"It can't be very comfortable," Winona thought. "If I had a pony, I'd teach him to sleep lying down. I'd want my pony very well took care of." She winked back tears.

Toodles, who had jumped up on her bed, began to whine, and Winona went over to him. He fell upon her, bouncing and sniffing and licking her hands and face. Winona pushed him off and he bounced back again. He barked and she laughed. It was fun.

"Yup!" said Winona, breathless from laughing. "Yup! Yup! I love you, Toodles. But I wish I had a pony. And I wish there were more than fifteen party invitations."

4

A Different Kind of
Party Invitation

AT SCHOOL the next afternoon Winona heard about a different kind of party invitation.

Miss Canning's room was the Third Grade. It was on the ground floor, and through the tall windows you could see the girls' yard, a sandy playground with two maple trees, good for playing

Prisoners Base. Their leaves were colored yellow now.

Dennie sat across the aisle from Winona, and that afternoon he gave her another stick of gum.

Winona was always glad to get gum; she wasn't allowed to chew it at home. Of course, she couldn't chew it in school either, but she could chew it at recess. She chewed this gum all through recess until the girls' line and the boys' line formed to march back into the school house. Then she stuck it on her signet ring. She squeezed it into a very tight ball and she thought it looked like a ruby.

But Miss Canning saw it and recognized it for gum. She took it away.

Dennie and Winona walked across the street to Winona's house together.

"That was good gum," Winona said. "I'd invite you to my birthday party, Dennie, only I haven't got any more invitations."

"Can't you just write some more?" he asked, sounding surprised.

"No. You see, my father had them printed down at the paper, and there were just fifteen, and my mother has sent them out to fifteen people. She's terribly sorry but there aren't any more."

"Heck!" said Dennie. "I don't need a printed invitation. You can just invite me, and I'll come."

"Will you?"

"Of course. When I have a birthday party, I don't print invitations or write invitations or stuff like that. My mother just tells me I can invite some kids and I invite them."

Winona gazed at him, her black eyes growing bigger and brighter.

"That's all there is to it," Dennie said. "I'd have asked you to some of my parties, Winona, but I've always had just boys. Maybe this year I'll have girls, too. I'll say to you, 'Say, can you come to a birthday party at my house tomorrow?' and you'll say sure, you can come."

They had reached her wall. Toodles was waiting for her, as he always did, wagging his tail and wriggling all over with pleasure.

"Toodles always seems to be waiting for you here," Dennie remarked.

"Yes," answered Winona. "He is. Toodles knows just as well as anybody does when school is over. Toodles is smart."

But she wasn't thinking about Toodles.

"Say, Dennie," she said carelessly, "can you come to my birthday party?"

"When's it going to be?"

"Next Thursday afternoon at half-past three."

"Sure, I'll come," he answered. "I'll bring a present, too."

After Dennie ran off down the hill, Winona stood smiling broadly. This was glorious! Dennie's way of inviting people to parties settled all her problems.

When Scundar and Marium came toiling up the hill, Winona called out to them.

"I'm giving a birthday party. Next Thursday afternoon at half-past three. Can you come?"

They were surprised but very, very pleased.

"We would be honored," said Scundar, taking off his hat.

"We are full of thanks to you," Marium exclaimed. Her small face was as bright as the scarf tied over her head. But after a moment it dimmed.

"I *think* I can come," she said. "But in the afternoon my mother goes out selling the embroideries. My Aunt Almaze takes care of my little brother Faddoul until I get home from school, but then *I* take care of him." She looked worried.

"Why, bring him to the party!" cried Winona hospitably.

Marium breathed deeply. "Would that be all right?"

"Of course! Bring him! Bring him!" Winona urged.

When Lottie and Lettie brought the laundry back, Winona invited them.

"I'm giving a birthday party. Can you come?"

The twins looked at each other and smiled. Their smiles would have been exactly alike except that Lottie had just lost two front teeth, and Lettie's matching ones were only loose. She wiggled them all the time so they would hurry and come out like Lottie's. But she stopped wiggling them now.

"Oh! Oh! We'd love to!" she cried.

"When's it going to be?" asked Lottie.

"Next Thursday afternoon at half-past three."

Winona invited people and invited people. She invited Betsy, Tacy, and Tib when they came to make the leaf house. They accepted promptly, but Betsy looked a little puzzled.

"Don't you send out invitations to your birthday parties?" she asked.

"Oh! Sometimes I do," said Winona airily. "And sometimes I don't. It's an awful bother. If you send out invitations, somebody has to print them, and somebody has to address them, and you have to decide how many kids you're going to have. Just asking people is lots easier."

They all agreed.

"Well, I'm practically sure we can come," said Betsy. "When is it?"

"Next Thursday afternoon at half-past three."

They ran down the terrace and scuffled through the leaves that covered the lower lawn. Toodles ran

after them, yelping joyfully. Fat squirrels with plumy tails dodged each other on the branches, and blue jays were flashing about.

The girls ran out to the barn and Ole gave them rakes. Ole took care of the lawn in summer and the fires in winter and the horses all the year round.

Winona and Betsy, Tacy, and Tib began to rake.

They had a wonderful time making the leaf house. There were leaves of every kind and color. Oak leaves and maple leaves and elm tree leaves. Orange-brown and red-brown and pink and pure gold and red and yellow and green.

Winona and Betsy, Tacy, and Tib raked them into walls. They made a parlor and a back parlor and a dining room and a kitchen and bedrooms.

Tib put lots of closets in the bedrooms.

"People never have enough closets. That's what my father says," she declared.

They made a porch. And Winona ran up to the side porch of her house and picked a piece of bright red vine to drape around the leaf house porch.

That gave Betsy an idea. She picked some of Mrs. Root's frostbitten zinnias. (Winona said she might.) She and Tacy stuck them in a row along the front of the leaf house.

"I want a barn!" Winona cried. So they raked some more leaves and made a barn. As soon as it was finished they sat down in the middle of it and started to talk about Winona's pony.

They all believed in the pony now. Or if they didn't, they pretended they did, which made it just as nice.

"Let's play a game of Naming the Pony," said Betsy. So they began.

Winona suggested Dolly because she liked that name. But Tib didn't want it, because she had an aunt named Dolly.

"It wouldn't be respectful to name your pony Dolly," she objected.

Betsy suggested Dixie and Tacy suggested Trixie. Tib suggested Buster, because of Buster Brown.

Winona suggested Sparkle; she had heard of a pony named Sparkle.

"Once," said Betsy, "I heard of a pony named Question because he had a question mark on his face."

"But maybe my pony won't have a question mark!" Winona protested.

Tacy suggested Dumpling. "That would be very good if he's fat," she pointed out.

Tib suggested Sugar because she knew ponies like sugar.

"They like carrots, too. But Carrots would be a funny name."

"Hay would be a funny name."

"Oats would be a very funny name!" Tacy shouted.

They were all laughing now. Tacy's face was red from laughter, and her blue eyes were streaming.

"You could name him Buffalo Bill," shrieked Tib, "because he kissed you one time!"

Winona pushed her into the leaves. Betsy and Tacy pounced upon Winona, and they all rolled over and over, screaming. Toodles barked and raced about.

It was a very humorous game.

When Mrs. Root called Winona in to practice her music lesson, Winona's face was shining with delight. It was dirty, though, and her mother sent her to wash it.

While she was washing, Winona thought and thought about how she could get a pony.

She went into her mother's bedroom, across the hall from the library. This was a beautiful room, with a canopy bed. The bed was white iron with a gleaming brass rail and pale green decorations, and the canopy stretched above like an awning. It had ruffles of white silk and pale green chiffon. The dressing table and bureau were white; so were the chairs; and all of them decorated in pale green. At the foot of the bed was a large white bearskin rug.

Mrs. Root sat by a window, mending.

"Mother," said Winona, holding out her hands so her mother could see how clean they were, "if I got a pony I wouldn't ride him bareback. I'd hitch him up to a little cart. I could act very dignified in a little pony cart."

Her mother finished sewing on a button. She snapped off some thread.

"Now be sure to practice half an hour," she said.

Winona went into the parlor because that was where the piano stood. The parlor wasn't so cozy as the library. Everything here was upholstered in rose pink. It had to be kept clean.

The upright piano had a rose pink scarf across the top. It had a stool to sit on. Winona had to whirl the stool to make it the proper height. Sometimes she whirled it and whirled it just to use up time when she was supposed to be practicing.

Today she didn't whirl a minute longer than she had to. As soon as the stool was high enough, she sat down and began to practice.

There was a clock beside the piano and Winona was supposed to practice half an hour. Sometimes if she got very tired or was very anxious to get outdoors and play, Winona would push the minute hand just a little bit ahead. After a little while, she would push it again.

"This clock is always gaining time," Winona often heard her mother say. Mr. Root took it to the jewelry store one time. He told the jeweler that he wanted it fixed, but the jeweler couldn't find anything wrong.

Today Winona didn't push the clock ahead. She practiced and practiced.

"Did you hear me playing those scales?" she asked, when she got back to her mother's bedroom after she had finished. "Didn't they sound exciting? If Father knew how good I played, maybe he'd get me a pony."

Mrs. Root was mending a ripped seam. She said they were going to have peach cobbler for supper.

Winona stood swinging back and forth on the tips of her toes.

"I can peel potatoes," she remarked. "I peeled one one time. Would Selma like to have me help her peel potatoes, do you s'pose?"

She knew it wasn't likely. Selma knew how to peel potatoes and peel them fast. She didn't need any help from little girls.

Mrs. Root looked at Winona gravely. "Why do you want to help Selma?" she asked.

Winona glanced away, embarrassed. "Oh, I just thought . . . Father likes me to learn . . ."

Mrs. Root laid down her mending. She put her arm around Winona.

"Winona," she said, "I don't want you to keep asking your father for a pony. I don't want you to have a pony. I don't think it's best for you."

Winona pulled away. She put her fists in her eyes.

Her mother got up and walked across the room. She felt bad, too.

"Winona," she said. "You've outgrown your party dress. Miss Flanders is making you a new one. I was planning to surprise you, but I'm going to tell you *now*. It's red."

"Red!" Winona leaped to her mother's arms.

"Bright red," Mrs. Root said. "And it has a red sash, and you'll wear a red hair ribbon to match."

"Oh, goody, goody!" Winona cried. "Is it done yet? Can I see it?"

She danced around the beautiful white and green room.

"It won't be finished until the day before the party. But you can see it. You can go and try it on," Mrs. Root said.

She was smiling tremulously. It made her glad to see Winona happy.

Winona was very happy about having a red

dress. She talked about it all through supper. She didn't mention her pony and she tried not to think about him. That was hard, though.

In spite of herself Winona kept wondering whether to name him Dumpling, or Sparkle, or Buster, or Buffalo Bill.

5

Getting Ready for the Party

WINONA SAW her new red party dress the next day. She went with her mother to try it on at Miss Flanders' house. Miss Flanders' house was little, but on the outside it looked as dignified as though it were big. It had a tower on top, and curliques up in the gable, and blood-red glass framing the front door.

Inside, it didn't look dignified at all. The sewing machine was open. Chairs were heaped with half-made dresses. And the floor was strewn with pins and buttons and hooks and eyes and snips and scraps of cloth.

Miss Flanders didn't look dignified either.

"Sewing is such messy work," she always apologized as you came in. Wisps of grayish-brown hair fell down from her pompadour, and her shirt waists were continually pulling out of her skirts.

She was a good dressmaker, though.

Winona's dress was even more beautiful than she had imagined it would be. It had short, puffed sleeves, and the skirt was accordion-pleated below a wide sash. It was a lovely vivid red.

"Oh, Mother!" Winona exclaimed, parading up and down in front of Miss Flanders' mirror, which swung in a frame and was long enough so you could see yourself from top to toe. "Oh, Mother! It's lovely! I look just like a gypsy!"

Mrs. Root looked at Miss Flanders and sighed. "Well, if you and your father are happy, I am!" she said.

"I'm sure," Miss Flanders put in brightly, "it's going to be a wonderful party!"

"Oh, it is! It is!" Winona whirled. The accordion-pleated skirt swelled out like a balloon. "Joyce can come," she added.

Joyce lived a long way away on the other side of town. She went to a different school, and Winona didn't see her very often.

Joyce had telephoned to say that she could come. It had made Winona feel very important to get a telephone call. Not many people in Deep Valley had telephones in their homes; these inventions were too new. But Mr. Root had one at home, as well as in his office, because he was editor of the *Deep Valley Sun*. And Joyce's father had one in his store. So Joyce had gone to his store to telephone Winona.

The other fourteen children who had received the printed cards wrote notes to Winona, or their mothers did. Everyone was pleased to accept her kind invitation.

Betsy, Tacy, and Tib could come. They had told Winona so at school. Their mothers had been a little surprised, Betsy said, that they hadn't received regular invitations.

"What did you tell them?" Winona asked.

"Oh," answered Betsy, "we explained that you were just asking people. I told my mother that Tacy and Tib were invited and *they* didn't have any invitations."

"And I told *my* mother that Betsy and Tib were invited and *they* didn't have any invitations," Tacy said.

"And I told *my* mother that Betsy and Tacy were invited and *they* didn't have any invitations," said Tib.

"That made everything perfectly all right, Winona," Tacy assured her kindly.

Dennie wanted to know what games they were going to play. He wanted to know whether they were going to have prizes. Winona asked her mother, and she said that they were.

Every day after school when the Syrian children came toiling up the hill, they stopped to talk about the party. They didn't go to many American parties.

"My little brother Faddoul says 'party, party, party' all day long," Marium chattered. She pronounced it 'par-r-rty,' for the Syrians always rolled their *r*'s. It made the word sound very exciting.

"See you Thursday if we live," Marium and Scundar called gaily as they departed. They didn't expect to die; that was just a Syrian saying.

Lottie and Lettie came up to Winona's house although they didn't have a basket to deliver or one to collect. They didn't even do tricks. They just sat on the lawn and talked about the party.

"Mamma is washing and ironing our party dresses and putting on new ribbons," Lottie sang.

"Hers are pink and mine are blue," sang Lettie.

"And we're going to wear white shoes. Mamma bought us some!"

Everyone was in a joyful dither.

The party came nearer and nearer all the time. And the trees grew more golden, and the vines grew redder.

"All getting ready for Winona's birthday!" her father kept on saying.

"And my dress will fit right in!" Winona cried. She was thrilled about the new red dress. She had told everyone at school about it. How red it was! How it flew out when she whirled!

But she still talked about the pony.

She didn't mention him to her father any more. And, of course, she didn't mention him to her mother. She didn't even mention him to Bessie and Myra. But to everybody else she did.

She and Betsy and Tacy and Tib tried to decide whether Winona should ride astride or sidesaddle, or whether she should have a pony cart.

"With a pony cart you could take more people riding," Betsy pointed out.

Dennie said jubilantly that with her pony and

Toodles she could give a dog and pony show, like Gentry's Dog and Pony Show that came to Deep Valley every summer.

"That's right!" Winona cried. "Of course we could! Lottie and Lettie could do tricks."

She told the postman that she was going to get a pony. She told the milkman and the baker's boy. It seemed as though, if she told enough people, she would make it come true.

She told the lamplighter who was a special friend of hers. Every night he came up the hill with his ladder. He set it against the lamp post on the corner and climbed up to light the lamp. His name was Mr. Dollar.

"Mr. Dollar," Winona said, "I'm going to get a pony."

"Is that a fact?" he asked.

"Yup!" She crossed her fingers behind her back, because, of course, it wasn't a fact, exactly.

And yet that pony got realer all the time.

Every spare minute Winona went down to the barn. She had always loved the barn, with its smell of hay and leather and the sounds Bob and Florence made, chewing and stamping in their stalls.

Winona went to the empty stall where her pony would live. It would need some nice clean straw on the floor, she decided.

"What's all this talk about a pony?" Ole asked. He was a bald, thin little man with blue eyes as faded as his overalls. "You're not going to get a pony. If you were, I'd be the first to hear of it."

"If I got one," Winona said, "he wouldn't be any work for you, Ole. I'd brush him and curry him and exercise him and bring him nice cold water."

"Ponies can't have cold water," Ole interrupted sourly.

Winona asked why not. And she asked how much hay a pony ought to get, and how much oats.

"Not many oats," Ole replied. "It makes them too frisky."

"But I *want* my pony frisky!" Winona insisted.

By and by Ole grew interested in the pony. He started telling Winona stories about ponies he had known.

Once a pony he was taking care of got into a field of buckwheat. He ate so much buckwheat that it made him blow up. Ole was able to save him from an early grave.

Another pony, named Traveler, knew how to get out of his pasture.

Traveler liked to go to the house next door because the lady there always gave him sugar. He would get out of his pasture, although the gate was closed, and go over and paw on her door. And when he had eaten his sugar he would go back to the pasture. He would get back in the same way he had gotten out.

"But how had he gotten out?" Winona demanded.

Ole put on his you'll-never-believe-this voice. "He'd crawl under the fence like a dog," he declared.

That same pony had a kitten for a friend. She would rather sleep in the barn with Traveler than in the house, Ole said. She slept in the straw in a corner of his stall. She liked to eat and drink with him and she never left his pasture in summer.

"Ya," said Ole, "she used to sit on a fence post with her four little paws as close together as though they were tied. Traveler would lean against the post, and they'd stay like that for half an hour. You'd swear they were talking."

Winona, who had climbed to the edge of the manger, bounced up and down.

"Oh, maybe my pony and Toodles will be friends like that!" she cried.

But then Ole told her again that she wasn't going to get a pony, and Winona walked slowly back into the house.

She found Bessie painting place cards for the party.

"Sixteen of them!" she said, laying the last one

aside to dry. They were pretty cards with pictures of birthday cakes on them.

But just sixteen! Winona looked at them uneasily.

"Maybe you ought to make a few extra, Bessie," she suggested. "There might be a few extra children."

"Why, no!" Bessie answered. "There can't be. There are only fifteen invited."

Myra showed her the favors. Sixteen paper hats and sixteen little tin horns.

"Do you have any extra ones?" Winona asked.

"Of course not! Why should we have extra ones?" Myra replied.

Winona was a little worried. Maybe she ought to tell someone about those children she'd invited? Or maybe it would be better not to.

Maybe it would just be borrowing trouble, she thought. She had heard her father say that.

And just then her mother asked her whether she would like to see the prizes.

She was allowed to see them because she couldn't possibly win one. She was the hostess. And even if she pinned the tail on the donkey on the exact spot where it was supposed to go, she couldn't win a prize. She'd have to give it to the child who had come next closest. Her mother had explained this to her.

There was a little iron cookstove for the girl's

prize—a real one; you could cook on it. The boy's prize was a bat and ball. Dennie would like a bat and ball, Winona thought with satisfaction.

"Oh, I can hardly wait for my birthday!" she cried, and her mother and Bessie and Myra smiled at each other.

"Fortunately," her mother said, "it's just day after tomorrow."

The next day, after school, Bessie and Myra gave Toodles a bath. Winona helped, of course. They didn't bathe him often; they didn't need to.

"Pug dogs are just naturally clean," Mrs. Root often said.

They bathed him in the kitchen, in his own round tub. Toodles didn't like to be bathed. He whined and snorted and tried to get out. Bessie held him while Myra scrubbed and Winona screamed and pranced.

First they put him into suds, and then they rinsed him, and then they dried him. It was easy to dry Toodles; his coat was so short.

After he was dry, they brushed him, and he acted pleased and strolled around with his tail curled tight as though he knew how nice he looked. His coat was like yellow satin; his ears were like black velvet.

"Oh, Toodles, you are beautiful!" Winona

exclaimed, and Myra and Bessie tied ribbons in his collar in honor of the party.

"Look at Toodles, Father!" Winona cried at supper.

Toodles ate beside her chair, from a low brown bowl. Mr. Root served him after he had served the family but before he served himself. Toodles got everything the family did, although Mrs. Root always protested. She thought he was too fat.

"But he does love to eat!" Bessie and Myra and Winona would plead. And Mr. Root kept on giving him tidbits.

Mr. Root regarded him admiringly now.

"Do you remember, Agatha," he asked his wife, "the night I brought Toodles home? I had asked Dr. Dodds to look up a pedigreed pug; you didn't know a thing about it. I brought him home in a baby's shoe box. He was just three weeks old."

Mother began to smile. "He was so dear!" she said. "He was the tiniest, softest, yellowest, loose-skinned, black-faced, pug-nosed little creature! Tiny as he was, he had those wrinkles. I didn't want you to have a puppy, Winona. I thought you were too young to take care of one properly. But when I saw him, I gave in."

"It was a good thing I surprised you," Mr. Root chuckled. He looked around the table. "Well, tomorrow I have a surprise for Winona!"

Winona put down her spoon in the midst of floating island. "A surprise? For me?"

"Who else is having a birthday?" her father teased. He was a tease like she was.

Winona thought fast. He had just been saying that Toodles was a surprise. Would this surprise be a pony?

She flashed a look toward her mother for if it was, her mother wouldn't like it. But Mrs. Root was smiling.

"Yes," she said. "Your father has a very nice idea."

This was discouraging. But the more Winona thought it over, the more it seemed to her that she must be getting a pony. A printing press wouldn't be a surprise. A big doll wouldn't be a surprise. A red silk dress wouldn't be a surprise. It must be a pony!

She tried to hide her joyful excitement. A surprise ought to be a surprise! She said, "Excuse me?" and burst out of the dining room and played with Toodles, singing loudly, "Won't you come home, Bill Bailey?" until her mother asked her please to stop singing that vulgar song.

Winona and Toodles went up to bed; and Myra came, too, and put Winona's hair up on rags for the party. She parted and combed the long, black locks and wet them and twisted them and wound them around the rags. Then she rolled the rags up tight and tied them in knots.

Winona looked in the mirror and howled with glee.

"You'll look pretty tomorrow," Myra said. "Prayers, now." And when prayers were over and Winona had hopped into bed, with Toodles settled at her feet, Myra kissed her goodnight. "Father's surprise . . . it's the cutest idea! I don't know how he ever thought of it," she said.

"*I* know how he thought of it," Winona said to herself. "He thought of it because I *asked* him for a pony, the night Mother addressed the party invitations."

She didn't say a word out loud, though, and Myra turned out the gas and went away.

Winona couldn't get to sleep. She was almost sure the surprise would be a pony. And yet . . . she couldn't be entirely sure.

She felt as though she were going up and down on a see-saw.

6

A Surprise for Mrs. Root

INONA WORE her hair in curls to school next day. And the Third Grade knew that her birthday had come at last. Miss Canning said, "Happy Birthday, Winona!" And all the children shouted, "Happy Birthday!"

Whenever a girl came to school looking particularly fancy, everyone knew that something was up.

Either she was giving a party or she was going to one. And in Winona's case there was no doubt about which it was. She had talked for days about her birthday.

Everyone knew that Betsy Ray must be going to the party, for her hair was not in its usual braids. It was curled to a friz.

"My sister Julia put it up on rags last night," Betsy told Winona at recess.

"My sister Myra put mine up on rags, too," Winona answered.

Winona and Betsy thought it was interesting that they each had two sisters and no brothers. They talked about it often.

Tacy's hair looked just as usual, and so did Tib's, for they had curls all the time. But they looked partyish, just the same; they looked so excited.

Dennie looked excited, too. After recess he leaned out to whisper to Winona.

"I hope there's plenty of birthday cake."

Winona nodded with gusto. Selma made wonderful birthday cakes, and Mrs. Root frosted them herself, putting on little birds and bouquets of flowers, and printing "Happy Birthday" in red candies.

It was hard that morning for Winona to keep her mind on arithmetic or geography or spelling. Her spelling was even worse than usual. Miss Canning, smiling, asked her to spell 'birthday' and Winona put in a *u* instead of an *i*.

In the afternoon she couldn't keep her eyes off the big clock on the wall. She wished she could fly up and push *that* minute hand ahead.

But at last, it pointed to three.

The Third Grade children went into the cloakroom for their jackets and caps, and then they formed lines. Someone played a march, as usual. The music always set Winona's feet to dancing, but today she positively jigged.

Birthday cake! Red silk dress! That surprise! *Could* it be a pony?

The marching lines went out the front door and down the steep steps into a crisp bright day.

"Ta ta! See you at my party!" Winona called to Betsy, Tacy, Tib, and Dennie, as she rushed across the school yard. They were rushing homeward, too. They had to change into their party clothes.

Toodles, waiting on the wall, was wearing his ribbons already. His tail seemed to be curled tighter than usual in honor of her birthday.

Inside the house there was a smell of freshly baked cake. And the dining room, when Winona peeked in, was a scene of gracious beauty. The long table was set with lace, candles, and flowers. There was a paper hat and a little tin horn at every place.

Of course—there were only sixteen places! Winona felt that pang of worry again.

"But it doesn't matter," she assured herself. "I can hold Joyce on my lap. And Lottie would just as soon as not hold Lettie. And Scundar and Marium could sort of squeeze in Marium's little brother."

She rushed upstairs.

"Be sure to wash," her mother called. "Myra," she added, "you'd better go and help her."

Bessie and Myra had hurried home from school in order to assist with the party.

Myra helped Winona wash her face and neck and ears. She helped her put on the new dress. It was like a dress out of a dream with its short puffed sleeves, and the wide sash, and the accordion-pleated skirt— all gloriously red.

Myra combed Winona's curls afresh and tied a red bow on the top of her head.

Winona rushed back downstairs and into her mother's bedroom. That was where her presents were always waiting, under the pale green canopy of Mother's bed. Her father was there. He had told her at breakfast that he would come home early.

"I'll be on hand," he had said. "I have to be . . . for that surprise."

He and her mother and sisters watched eagerly as Winona dashed for her presents.

There was the doll as big as a baby, jointed, with yellow hair and eyes that opened and shut. It was the doll she had asked for, the one her father had said he couldn't afford.

"Is this the surprise?" Winona asked.

Her father said no.

Beside the doll was a wardrobe full of doll clothes from her mother.

"Some of them are your own baby clothes," Mrs. Root said tenderly. "This doll is almost as big as you were when you were born, Winona."

Winona riffled through the doll clothes. "Are they the surprise?" she asked.

Her mother said no.

On the table beside the bed was a little printing press. It was just what Winona had wanted.

"Is this the surprise?" she asked.

"No, not that," her father answered. "The surprise is coming later, Win. It isn't a present, exactly."

Then it wasn't the hand-painted ribbon box from Bessie or the copy of *Black Beauty* from Myra. Winona hugged and kissed her sisters and her mother and father.

The doorbell rang.

"Why, it isn't half-past three yet," Mr. Root chuckled.

"Oh, they always come early," Mrs. Root laughed.

Winona flew to open the door. "It's Dennie!" she shouted.

Dennie looked very spruce in his blue Sunday suit with long, ribbed stockings and polished shoes. He wore a sateen blouse, striped blue and red, and a neat blue tie. His curly hair was brushed to a peak above a rosy face.

"Happy birthday! Here's my present," he said, extending a package.

It was a Noah's Ark.

"Watch me whirl!" cried Winona, and whirled to show him how her skirt flew out.

"Gee!" said Dennie. "You can wear that for the circus."

Winona's mother looked surprised to see Dennie. She looked very surprised. She didn't say anything, though.

In just a minute the doorbell rang again. This time it was Joyce, fat and jolly, her thick braid swinging. She said, "Happy Birthday!" and gave Winona a cup and saucer. Winona whirled for her, and they jumped about for joy.

A girl from Winona's Sunday School class came next, bringing a game of Authors. A carriage stopped outside and Percy came in.

His blond curls were neat as usual, and he wore a velvet suit and a waist with a ruffled collar and ruffles down the front.

"Who's that sissy?" Dennie whispered to Winona.

"My mother knows his mother," Winona whispered back.

Percy brought a bouquet of flowers in a holder.

"My mother bought it," he said crossly, thrusting it at Winona. He walked to the window and looked out, acting haughty. Nobody followed him.

After that, children came in a steady stream. Each one said, "Happy Birthday!" and gave Winona a present. The presents were unwrapped and put on that table in her mother's room where the printing press was. Soon the beautiful white and green room was a sea of tissue paper, and the table was crowded with cups and saucers, silk embroidered handkerchiefs, games and books, a tea set, and a ring with three pearls and twelve rubies in it.

Lottie and Lettie brought a pair of mittens. They were red and green, with tassels.

"Mamma knitted them herself," Lottie said to Mrs. Root who was admiring them with a strange look on her face.

Lottie and Lettie looked nice in their starched white dresses. They looked a little summery, but the pink and blue ribbons streamed from rosettes on their shoulders. And they wore their new white shoes.

Winona saw her mother go out to the dining room. She picked up all the place cards and came back.

Betsy, Tacy, and Tib arrived together, each one with a present. Tacy stayed close to Betsy at first; she was bashful at parties. And none of them had been inside Winona's house before.

Betsy's party dress was brown, piped in pink. She, too, had an accordion-pleated skirt. Tacy's dress was dark blue silk with a tucked yoke of lighter blue. Tacy usually wore blue because she had red hair. Tib's pink wool dress was belted low; that was the newest style.

"My Aunt Dolly sent it to me from Milwaukee," she said, pirouetting.

That reminded Winona to whirl, so she whirled, and Betsy whirled, too. They whirled and whirled to see whose skirt would spread out the widest.

Winona's mother was looking absolutely mystified.

"Winona," she said, "won't you introduce me to your friends?" When she heard their names, she said faintly, "Oh, yes! I think I know your mothers."

Children came and came and came.

There was one little boy, five years old, who lived down the block; Winona took care of him sometimes. He was wearing a clean sailor suit.

Two other little boys, about his age, were wearing Indian suits. They thought it was a Halloween party!

Winona's father had disappeared. Her mother and sisters were whispering in a corner. Shortly her mother beckoned Winona to join them.

"Winona," she said, speaking gently, but with something urgent in her voice, "just how many children have you invited, dear? They're very welcome but I have to know how many there will be, on account of the refreshments."

"Won't there be enough ice cream . . . on my *birthday*?" Winona asked indignantly.

"We don't need to worry about the ice cream," her mother answered. "Myra will run down to the drug store and buy more. But it's hard to stretch a birthday cake."

"But Dennie especially asked about the cake! I told him we had plenty!" This was terrible.

Before Mrs. Root had a chance to answer, the doorbell rang a last time, and in came Scundar and Marium and Faddoul. Scundar looked very handsome. He was wearing a red tie, and his black hair was plastered down with oil.

Marium looked like a picture out of *The Arabian Nights*, in a purple dress, very long and full. She was wearing purple ribbons on her long, black braids, and earrings, and even more bracelets than usual. Her eyes were rimmed with something black which was very becoming.

"Happy Birthday," she said like everyone else. She was holding her little brother tightly by the hand.

Faddoul was very chubby with fat red cheeks. His eyes were like ripe olives as he stared around the house. Marium nudged him, and he murmured something and gave Winona a box of candied fruit.

Marium's package held a handmade lace doily. It was exquisite, Bessie said.

Scundar balanced his gift carefully on outstretched hands. He carried it over to Mrs. Root who was looking more and more amazed all the time. In fact, she was looking pale.

"My mother hopes you will like this poor baklawa cake," Scundar said, and bowed.

"Cake!" cried Mrs. Root in a tone of thankfulness.

"Cake!" cried Winona and hurried over to look. It was an odd but delicious-looking cake, crisscrossed like a checkerboard and oozing honey.

"Oh, Mother!" cried Winona. "Now there'll be plenty of cake!"

"Yes," said Mrs. Root, "thanks to this Syrian mother!"

"Oh, the Syrians are lovely people!" cried Winona, dancing about.

The children were all looking at her presents. Betsy was charmed by the printing press.

"I'm going to get out a newspaper for children," Winona said importantly.

"Can I write stories for it?" Betsy asked.

"I could make you a funny paper," offered Tib. "I can draw Buster Brown and Happy Hooligan and the Katzenjammer Kids."

"I could peddle the papers," chimed in Tacy. She wasn't feeling bashful any more.

Lottie and Lettie liked the big doll. Winona told them they could undress it and put on different clothes. So they did, while Marium watched admiringly.

The boys were asking when the games would begin.

Nobody asked about the pony. Perhaps, Winona thought, they had forgotten about him in the excitement of the party. Perhaps they were being polite, or perhaps they had thought all along that the pony was just a sort of game.

But Winona didn't forget him. She couldn't help expecting him. After all, she hadn't had the surprise!

They went into the library, and she pointed out

that picture she liked. It was the one an artist had painted down at her father's office, showing a copy of the *Deep Valley Sun*, and a cigar, and a violin, and a mouse.

"What do you s'pose that mouse is doing there?" Winona asked the company.

"I could make up a story about it," Betsy volunteered. "You could print it on your printing press."

"Do it now!" Winona commanded. But there wasn't time. Her mother had started blindfolding children for Pin the Tail on the Donkey. Lottie won the cookstove, and Dennie won the bat and ball. Winona was glad about that.

Afterward, they ran out to the lower lawn for London Bridge. After that they played Go In and Out the Window. And then Lottie and Lettie did some of their tricks. Lettie stood on Lottie's shoulders. They were acrobats, practically.

Little Faddoul had a good time rolling down the terrace.

He would lie down with his arms at his sides, making a fat little bundle. And he would roll over and over, down the steep slope to the bottom, where he ended in a nest of colored leaves. Then he would get up solemnly and climb to the top of the terrace and roll down again. Toodles followed him, barking, because he liked that game.

The little boy in the sailor suit was busy count-ing leaves. He could only count to ten. When he reached ten he would start all over again.

The two little boys dressed like Indians were playing by themselves, giving war whoops and wav-ing sticks that they pretended were tomahawks.

Winona kept looking around for her father. Where was he? And what was the surprise?

Her mother and Bessie and Myra seemed to be looking for him, too . . . or for something. They kept rushing out to the barn. Even Ole acted queer.

He had marked out a white circle on the lower lawn with ground lime. It was big, something like a race track.

"What game is this for, Ole?" Winona asked. But he wouldn't answer.

Instead, he yelled to the children to stand back.

"Back! Back! Behind that circle," he yelled.

"Stand back, children!" Winona's mother echoed, lifting her long skirts and running to and fro.

When everyone had crowded back, Ole turned toward the barn. He opened the gate that led to the corral where he exercised Florence and Bob. He opened it wide, and Winona's father came out, smiling.

"Winona!" he called. "Here is your surprise!"

7

A Surprise for Winona

WINONA STOOD staring at the gate of the corral. Something funny was happening inside of her. Something had swelled up and was pushing into her throat. She wanted to cry, but she wouldn't, of course. Not any more than she had when Buffalo Bill kissed her.

She knew that a pony would come through the gate, and he did.

First she heard a jingling of little bells, then the beat of tiny hoofs. Then the pony trotted out, hitched to a pony cart. It was a small wicker cart with red wheels and two seats, set back to back.

The man who held the reins wasn't sitting in the cart. He was running along beside the pony, laughing.

"Giddap, Jingle! Giddap, Jingle!" he was calling in a laughing voice. He was a thin young man with reddish hair, and he was wearing a green velvet jacket.

Winona looked at him and at the cart because she could hardly bear to look at the pony. It made her too glad.

At last, she stole a fearful glance.

He was a stocky shaggy little pony. He was black, but his bushy forelock, mane, and tail were white. Later Winona was to discover that he had a little chocolate on one ear and a little vanilla on the other; that was a joke she made up.

Now she noticed chiefly that his ears stood up jauntily and his eyes were large and bright. His tail was lifted gaily as though he enjoyed coming to a party.

"Giddap, Jingle!" the young man kept crying.

Jingle! Winona looked toward Betsy, Tacy, and Tib. They needn't have bothered trying so hard to think of a name for her pony. He had brought his own name—Jingle, like his little jingling bells.

Jingle came straight to Winona and stopped. The young man smiled and put the reins into her hands.

"Jingle, at your service, miss!" he said, touching his cap.

Winona couldn't speak.

Her father came up. He looked pleased with himself.

"Wasn't this a nice surprise?" he asked. "I thought you might like to have a pony come to your party and give the children rides."

"Father!" cried Winona. She dashed into his arms and rubbed her eyes on the sleeve of his coat so that no one would see they were wet.

"Who will you choose to take for the first ride?" her mother asked. She was smiling, too. Her mother didn't mind after all, Winona thought, because her father had given her a pony!

There was no doubt about whom she would choose.

"Joyce!" she called, and Joyce ran over, her butter-colored braid swinging proudly.

"There's room for two more," the young man said.

"Anybody!" Winona yelled. There was a wild rush, but Tib and Dennie reached the pony cart first. They clambered up into the back seat.

The young man took the reins again, and Winona and Joyce climbed into the front seat. The cushions were black, tufted with red. The whip was red.

"That whip is just for decoration, miss," the young man warned with a wink of his blue eye. "Jingle doesn't like the whip."

"He doesn't like the whip whatsoever!" Winona shouted to her interested guests.

She didn't feel at all like crying any more. She took the reins back and sat up straight and looked around radiantly at the crowding, clamoring children.

"Just touch him with the reins when you want him to start," the young man said.

"Drive him around that track," her father directed, pointing to the circle Ole had marked out. He was as excited as Winona was, almost.

"Ya, but I'll lead him the first time," Ole cut in. He was excited, too.

Toodles was most excited of all. He had come rushing down from the terrace to see what was going on, but when he found Winona sitting in the pony cart looking such a picture of bliss, he didn't seem to like it. He began to bark furiously. He ran around the pony, barking.

"Better put Toodles in the house," Mr. Root said.

"He might make the pony nervous."

So Myra picked him up and carried him in. She told him severely that he must be good.

"Toodles will get to like Jingle soon," Winona thought. "He'll like him as well as that kitten Ole told me about liked the pony named Traveler."

"All set?" her father asked.

Winona nodded, her eyes like black stars. She slapped the reins gently on Jingle's back.

"Giddap, Jingle!" she said.

Jingle started to walk around the circle. The bells on his harness jingled merrily. After the first round, Ole let go of the bridle, and Jingle broke into a merry little trot. When he had gone around three times, he stopped.

"Me, next! No, me! Me! Me!" the children clamored, swarming around the pony cart.

"Remember me, Winona!"

"I'm your friend, Winona!"

Mrs. Root was afraid that someone would get hurt. But no one did. And everyone got a ride . . . except Faddoul, who didn't want one. He was having too much fun rolling down the terrace.

Scundar and Marium got a ride, and the little boy in the sailor suit, and all the girls from Winona's Sunday School class. The little boys dressed as Indians stopped being Indians long enough for a ride.

Lottie and Lettie waved to the crowd. Betsy and Tacy sat close together, holding hands. Percy had been acting stand-offish all afternoon but he cheered up after Jingle came. He smiled as Winona drove him briskly around the circle.

Winona didn't always drive. She didn't even always ride. There were too many children screaming and waving and jumping for their turn. And she was hostess, her mother reminded her gently. Winona didn't mind.

"I can drive him tomorrow," she thought, climbing out. "And the day after that."

She liked to watch the shaggy little pony pulling the cart around and around under the bright trees.

Jingle didn't seem to mind how many times he went around. He seemed to be used to giving children rides.

"He likes children," Winona thought. And so did the young man in the green velvet coat. She wondered whether he used to own Jingle. He understood him pretty well.

"Would you like to have me unhitch the pony?" the young man asked Mr. Root. "Let the youngsters ride?"

"A fine idea!" Mr. Root replied. "I'll give them some lessons." Winona's father knew how to ride very well.

The young man unhitched Jingle and put a blanket on his back, and then a saddle. But when Mr. Root came up, Jingle turned around and looked at him. He put his ears back. He acted cross.

"Jingle won't let a man ride him," the young man said. "He doesn't like men, except me."

"He doesn't like men!" Winona shouted to the crowd. "He doesn't like men whatsoever!"

"He's always all right with children, though," the young man added.

"We'll let Winona try it then," her father said, and Winona skipped joyfully over to Jingle. She climbed into the saddle and put her feet in the stirrups.

Jingle walked around the circle, cheerful once more.

Tib rode next, as triumphantly as Winona. Tacy acted a little timid; she rode round the circle, though.

When Betsy's turn came, she said, "Thank you very much. Just a *little* ride, please."

She was slow getting on. And once on Jingle's back, she refused the bridle.

"I'll just ride this way," she said, putting her arms tightly around the pony's neck. Jingle didn't seem to mind, but after a few steps he paused.

Betsy scrambled off.

"You didn't get all your ride!" Winona protested. "Get back on!" she added generously. "You can go around three times."

But Betsy backed hurriedly away. "Oh, I got plenty. Thank you. It was lovely," she said.

Most of the children seemed a little in awe of Jingle. And no one knew exactly how to ride. Mr. Root shouted directions from the sidelines, but he only confused them.

Nothing confused Jingle. He trotted around and around in his usual business-like way . . . until Percy's turn came.

Percy climbed on, and he seemed to know exactly what to do. He lifted the reins commandingly and pushed his knees into the pony's sides. Perhaps he rode like a man.

At any rate, Jingle turned around and looked at Percy. He looked at him just as he had looked at Mr. Root. He put his ears back. He acted cross. And then like lightning he bolted the track Ole had marked out on the lawn and headed for the alley.

There was an uproar.

"Wow! Look at that!"

"Help! Help!"

"God save!" cried Scundar and Marium.

Bessie and Myra ran to their mother. Mr. Root and the red-haired young man raced in pursuit of the pony.

Winona jumped up and down in a panic. She didn't mind having Jingle run away. It was thrilling to have a wild pony. But that Percy, of all people, should be on his back in this moment of danger! Percy, with his curls and velvet suit and ruffled blouse!

"Percy will faint dead away!" Dennie said.

But Percy didn't.

As Jingle galloped down the alley, Percy kept his seat. He wasn't, Winona saw with amazement, even tugging on the reins. Jingle galloped and galloped, his white tail flying, but Percy held him firmly and at last even succeeded in turning him around.

Mr. Root and the red-haired young man had almost reached them, but Jingle veered away into somebody's back lawn. Still Percy kept his seat and held the reins.

Jingle kept galloping, but at least he was galloping in the right direction now. He galloped from lawn to lawn, stepping into flower beds now and then, dodging a big bonfire in which a neighbor of the Roots was burning leaves!

At last he reached the lawn of the house next door.

There was a low hedge between that lawn and the lower lawn of the Root house. Jingle jumped. He went up and over in a stunning leap, and Percy didn't fall off. He bent low like a cowboy. His yellow curls were blowing. He was smiling.

Once across the hedge on the Root lawn, Jingle stopped. He stood still and put his head down, acting ashamed. Percy jumped off and patted him, and Jingle nuzzled Percy's arm.

Everyone crowded around, shouting and exclaiming.

"Percy!" cried Winona. "You were perfectly wonderful!"

"Maybe you'll ride in a circus we're going to have!" Dennie urged.

"You certainly know how to ride," said the young man in the green velvet coat, running up out of breath.

Mr. Root clapped Percy on the back. "Your father would have been proud of you, son," he said.

Winona looked at Percy, thinking hard.

"Maybe," she thought, "if I were a boy, Mother would make *me* wear a ruffled blouse."

No one else rode Jingle after that. Instead they fed him sugar and carrots. Selma brought out an apple, and he ate that. They picked some clover, and he ate that.

"He'll eat anything," the young man laughed. "He even eats ice cream."

"He shall have some then," Mrs. Root said kindly.

"Children!" she called. "It's time for refreshments!"

Bessie had started playing the piano, and Myra formed the party into a line. They marched around the house and into the front door. They must be going to the dining room, Winona thought, and she could not help feeling a little anxious.

They could hold each other on their laps, of course. And her mother had taken off the place cards. But there were only sixteen caps and sixteen tin horns!

To her great relief they didn't go into the dining room after all.

They went into the library, where sheets had been spread on the carpet. They sat down in a circle, and Bessie and Myra passed dishes of ice cream. There was plenty of ice cream because Myra had gone down to the drug store and bought more.

Winona's mother came in carrying the birthday cake. It was a beautiful cake with little birds and bouquets of flowers in the frosting. Everyone sang "Happy Birthday" and Winona blew the candles out. But she didn't know what to wish for because now she had a pony.

The cake wasn't enormously big for so very many children but it didn't matter. Right behind Mrs. Root came Bessie with the cake Scundar had brought.

"There's going to be lots of cake," Mrs. Root said, "because Scundar brought Winona this beautiful present."

The baklawa cake was rich and sweet, covered with honey. It was delicious.

Everything turned out all right.

It was even all right about the favors. There were just sixteen caps and sixteen tin horns but instead of giving each one a cap and a horn, Mrs. Root gave each one a cap *or* a horn. Everyone got something, and they had fun exchanging.

Toodles came out from under the lounge. The children played with him and gave him bites. They talked about the pony.

Joyce said she would rather have the big, jointed doll.

"And I'd rather have the printing press," said Betsy, looking thoughtfully at that picture with the mouse.

Scundar looked up at the sparkling chandelier hanging from the ceiling.

"How do you light it?" he wanted to know.

Winona showed him the lighter, a long-handled stick with a taper in the end. You lighted the taper, then turned on the gas with the stick and lighted the gas with the taper.

Lottie and Lettie went out in the hall to look at

the telephone. The long, dark box was attached to the wall, with a bell on one side that you cranked to get Central.

"If Mamma had a telephone we'd telephone her," Lettie cried.

At last the doorbell began ringing. Parents were coming to take their children home. Children who lived near enough to go home alone ran into the bedroom for their jackets. They all told Mrs. Root they had had a nice time.

"We are full of thanks to you," Scundar said, bowing, and Marium added demurely, "You are welcome at our home at any time."

Winona's mother looked at them with a wondering smile.

"Pro'bly," Winona thought, "she didn't know Syrians were so nice."

Mrs. Root thanked them again for the cake. She thanked Lottie and Lettie again for the mittens.

Betsy, Tacy, and Tib left together, hand in hand.

Usually Winona hated to have a party end, but she was glad tonight when the last child was gone. Now she could take some ice cream out to Jingle. She could hardly wait to see him again.

Her mother sat down on the lounge. "Winona dear," she began. "Come here! I want to talk to you."

But Winona ran toward the kitchen pretending that she hadn't heard. She did so want to see Jingle! And the talk would only be about those children she had invited to the party.

"Winona!" Mrs. Root repeated, and then Winona came back and sat down. She had to, when her mother used that tone. She kept thinking about Jingle, though.

Her mother took hold of Winona's hand and looked at her for a long time without saying a word.

"I'm not going to punish you," she said at last, "because it's your birthday, but I want to be sure you understand what a foolish, thoughtless thing you did. Why, we might not have had enough ice cream! We might not have had enough cake! Even as it was, you caused great inconvenience. All those beautiful place cards Bessie made were wasted! And she had worked on them so hard!"

Winona hadn't thought of that. She was sorry.

"I hope," Mrs. Root said gravely, "you will be more thoughtful, Winona, now that you are eight."

Winona bounded upright.

"That's right," she thought to herself, "I *am* eight. Eight years old!" She'd been too busy with the party and the pony to think about it before.

"Oh, Mother!" she cried. "I'm sure I will! I'll be

more thoughtful . . . and more ladylike . . . and more . . . more . . . dignified. I did such foolish things when I was only seven, Mother. It's different now that I'm eight."

Her mother said she hoped so.

"Now may I go?" Winona asked, swinging on her toes.

"Where do you want to go?"

"Why, to take . . ." But suddenly Winona decided not to stop to get ice cream. Her mother might think it was too late to go outdoors, or that she ought to put on a jacket or something. Her mother wouldn't understand—nobody could—how much she wanted to see Jingle in his own little stall.

"I'll be back in a sec," Winona cried.

She ran through the kitchen and out into the twilight.

8
Winona and Jingle

IT WAS growing dark outside. Mr. Dollar had lighted the street lamp. A wind had come up and was bringing down the leaves. They had almost covered the track Ole had laid out that afternoon.

Winona hurried into the barn. She was cold in her party dress. And Jingle, she thought, had better have a blanket. She wanted to get to him quickly, to pet him. He was such a little pony! He might feel lonesome the first night in his new home.

She passed Bob and Florence in their stalls. They stopped eating their oats and turned their heads to look at her. But the empty stall which she had planned would be Jingle's was empty still. Ole hadn't even put fresh straw on the floor.

And where was Ole? He wasn't in the barn. He wasn't in the corral. Winona ran out into the alley. And there she saw the young man in the green velvet coat leading Jingle down toward Pleasant Street.

"Wait! Wait!" Winona ran after him as fast as her legs would carry her. The wind whipped the skirts of her accordion-pleated dress.

"What's the matter, little girl?" the young man asked.

She looked at him with imploring black eyes and caught Jingle's bridle.

"Why . . . what's up?" He was trying to joke.

"Where are you going with my pony?" Winona demanded.

The young man passed his hands over his red hair. With his smile gone, he looked tired and his expression was anxious.

"You don't understand," he said. "Your father hired me to bring Jingle this afternoon to entertain the children. Jingle is my pony."

"No! No!" Winona cried.

"I take him around from town to town so children can ride him. That's my business. When I reached Deep Valley yesterday I went to the *Sun* to put an ad in your father's paper . . ."

"No!" Winona stopped him. She began to cry wildly. "Father! Mother! Ole!"

Ole came running out of the kitchen, where he had been eating his supper. Selma ran out after him, her apron flying. Mr. and Mrs. Root, Bessie, and Myra came from the dining room through the back porch.

Winona flung herself into her father's arms, crying and sobbing.

She heard the young man say, "The little girl seemed to think the pony was hers. She didn't understand."

Her father hugged her and murmured comforting words. Winona heard him speak to the young man.

"Let the pony stay here tonight," he said in a low voice. "Ole can put him up in the barn. There's an empty stall."

An empty stall! Jingle wasn't supposed to sleep in it just one night. That was supposed to be his home, forever.

With her father and mother on either side and

her sisters behind, Winona went sobbing back into the house. In the library, she pulled away and threw herself down on the rug in front of the fire.

Toodles whined and licked her ear. He found her cheek and licked that. Winona put her arm around him, but she kept on crying.

Sometimes when Winona wanted something she cried in order to get it. She knew that wasn't a good thing to do. She felt ashamed after she did it. But that wasn't the way she was crying tonight. She was crying because she couldn't help it.

Her father and mother and Bessie and Myra tried to make her stop, but she couldn't.

"We'd better just leave her alone a few minutes," her father said.

"She's tired out from the party . . . all that excitement," said her mother.

"No," answered her father. "It's more than that."

They went to the end of the room and talked softly.

Winona's sobs grew quieter at last; she could hear what they were saying. It didn't seem important at first. It was like what you hear when you're half asleep and people are talking in another room. But it began to make sense.

"You know, Agatha," her father said, "a Shetland hasn't any vicious traits. He loves children and enters into their play just like another child."

"Winona has Toodles and two sisters to play with," Mrs. Root replied.

"A pony keeps a boy or girl out in the sunshine and fresh air," her father said. "It's a wonderful source of health."

"Winona is perfectly healthy," her mother answered. "And she's out of doors more than I want her to be."

"Owning a pony develops a sense of responsibility," her father said. "The child should take care of him, of course. Winona should be taught to feed and water him and to give him exercise. It would be good for her."

"Oh, Horace!" Mrs. Root cried despairingly. "You don't know the trouble I have making Winona ladylike. She isn't like the other girls. She's more like you."

"I had a pony," Mr. Root said. "I didn't grow up until I had a pony."

"But you were a boy! And a Westerner, too!"

Winona heard her father give a little laugh. She was listening hard now. She knew very well what was being decided. Maybe, she thought, she ought to pray. But she couldn't stop listening.

"Agatha darling," Mr. Root said, "you've never gotten over the feeling that when you came to

Minnesota, you came to the Wild West. But more ladies ride back East than they do here. You've seen them yourself in Central Park. Mrs. Vanderbilt, Mrs. Astor, Lillian Russell . . ."

Father's voice was teasing now; it seemed a little risky.

"Why, Queen Victoria rides!" he said. "Or she did when she was young."

"Mother," said Bessie, and Winona could tell from the sound of her voice that she was crying, "Winona could wear divided skirts."

"She could ride sidesaddle," pleaded Myra between sniffs. "Our minister would think it was all right. I'm sure he would."

"All I want," said Mrs. Root, "is what is best for Winona."

Her voice was trembling and Mr. Root answered gently, "Of course, dear! We all understand that. Well, you know more than I do about raising girls!"

There was silence.

It was decided, Winona realized feeling empty inside. She couldn't have a pony.

She didn't want to cry any more. She had cried all the tears she had. She had lost Jingle; that was all there was to it. But she would never forget him.

"I'll love him as long as I live," she thought. "I'll love him whether he's mine or not."

She remembered him trotting around and around under the red and yellow trees.

It had been a wonderful party, she thought, almost smiling. And after all she had her big doll. And the little printing press. They weren't as nice as Jingle but they were very nice. How Betsy Ray had liked that printing press!

Winona remembered the newspaper they were going to have. Betsy was going to write stories for it, and Tib was going to draw pictures, and Tacy was going to peddle the papers. She herself would be editor like her father.

"Maybe we'll make money enough to buy Jingle!" she thought, and jumped up, and dried her wet cheeks with her hands, and shook out the crumpled red dress.

She didn't really believe they would, but it was fun to pretend.

Her father and mother and Bessie and Myra were looking at her anxiously.

"Father," said Winona. "I'm going to get my printing press. Will you show me how it works?"

A smile broke over his face. "You bet I will, Win," he answered.

"What a little brick!" she heard him say as she went out. That made Winona feel proud.

She got the printing press from the bedroom

where her presents were arranged, and when she crossed the hall again she saw through the open library door that her father was walking up and down with his hands behind his back. He wasn't smiling any more.

"It was all my stupid fault!" he burst out unexpectedly, to Winona's surprise. "I should have told her the pony was just rented for the afternoon! I should have known what she'd think . . . after she'd asked me for a pony."

"So should I," said Mrs. Root. "She asked me, too. It was my fault, too."

Suddenly her voice took on a different tone. She sounded happy and excited.

"Horace!" she said. "Horace! Let her have the pony!"

Winona stood perfectly still. She had to. Her feet seemed to be rooted to the carpet. And something rushed over her; it was like a wind full of joy and love and gratefulness. She was grateful for everything—not just the pony. For the party, and her presents, and her father and mother and sisters.

"Winona!" her mother called.

"Come a-running, Win!" her father shouted.

Winona's feet came loose. She went a-running.

"Winona," her mother began, "we've decided. . . ."

But Winona interrupted. "Oh, Mother!" she cried.

"You don't need to tell me. I heard."

She threw her arms around her mother's neck and hugged her. She hugged with such violence, and her mother was so frail, that Winona almost knocked her over. But Mrs. Root seemed to like it. She hugged back.

"I'll ride sidesaddle, Mother," Winona cried. "I'll wear divided skirts. And I'll drive out in the little cart just like you and Bessie and Myra drive with Florence."

Her mother started to cry.

Winona flew to her father. She hugged him and kissed him and hugged him.

"Father," she said, "I'll learn to play the piano good. I'll never whirl the stool when I ought to be practicing, and I'll never, never push the clock ahead."

"Why, you little monkey!" said her father. "Is *that* what was the matter with that clock?"

Winona got up and danced around the room. She kissed Bessie. She kissed Myra. They looked funny with their faces streaked with tears when they were still wearing their party dresses. The library still looked like the party. The white sheet, full of crumbs, was still on the floor.

Selma came to the door. She had been crying, too.

"Selma," Winona cried, running to hug her, "I

can keep Jingle! Jingle is my pony!"

Ole came running in, blowing his nose on a bright red handkerchief.

"Ole!" Winona cried. "I can keep Jingle. And he won't be a bit of trouble to you, Ole. I'll feed him and water him and curry him and clean out his stall. He'll give me a great sense of re-re-responsibility, Ole."

"Ya, ya!" Ole said.

"See here!" said her father. "You're going to have a pony. But maybe you don't want Jingle . . . he's had a hard life. He's gone around with that young man for years entertaining children."

Winona gazed at her father with black reproachful eyes. "Why, *of course* I want Jingle! He's my pony!" she said.

"Oh, all right, all right!" her father replied.

In the morning when the young man returned, Mr. Root bought Jingle and his harness and the pony cart. He wrote the young man a check.

"Glad to get it!" the young man said, looking at it with a pleased expression before he folded it up and put it in his pocket. "I've been wanting to get out of this business. I think I'll find a merry-go-round."

"I'll take good care of Jingle," Winona said.
And she did.

Ole insisted upon cleaning his stall. He thought Winona was pretty little to clean stalls. Besides, her mother didn't want her to do it. But Winona learned how to feed Jingle; she learned how to give him his oats and hay . . . and a little bran mash now and then.

She learned that his drinking water should be fresh but never cold and that she shouldn't feed or water him while he was hot. If he was warm when she brought him home, she unharnessed him and threw a blanket over him.

She learned how to brush him and curry him.

This wasn't easy in the winter. Then Jingle had a very heavy coat. It was almost waterproof. In the spring his shaggy coat hung in untidy rags and tatters. He would rub himself on the ground to try to get rid of part of it. Ole clipped him then, while Winona watched. He trimmed Jingle's white mane and tail.

In the summer Jingle's coat was shiny and handsome.

Winona learned how to harness him to the little cart. She learned how to saddle him. Jingle didn't like to be saddled.

"He doesn't like to be saddled whatsoever!" Winona would shout. For whenever she started to put on the saddle he would blow out like a balloon.

Later, of course, the girth wouldn't be tight enough.

Ole suggested giving him an apple when she came out to saddle him.

Jingle loved apples. In fact, as his late owner had said, he loved to eat. He would nose into people's pockets for sugar. He crunched on carrots with delight.

He loved freshly cut grass. He loved clover. He liked to graze on the lower lawn and nibble. But once he ate some little evergreens Mr. Root had bought to plant along the alley. Once he ate some flowers from Mrs. Root's garden. Once the baker's boy left four loaves of bread on the back porch, and Jingle chewed into them all.

He would go up to Selma's kitchen door and whinny, and Selma would say, "You're as bad as Toodles!" but she always found something for him to eat.

Jingle liked to come into the house. If he found a door open he would walk right in and down the front hall. Winona's mother didn't like that. Winona had to train him not to do it.

Toodles didn't like it either.

Toodles loved the pony cart, though. He was so fat that Winona had to lift him in and out, but he would ride contentedly for hours. He would sit beside her looking around at the streets, with his tail curled as tight as a doughnut.

He never came to love Jingle as much as that kitten loved the pony named Traveler. Toodles wouldn't have liked sleeping in the barn. He liked to sleep with Winona. And when winter came he liked to lie by the fire. But he did love riding in the pony cart.

Sometimes Winona used to drive up to the high school to call for Bessie and Myra. She would wait for them out in front, sitting up straight, holding the whip in her hand. Of course, she never used it.

Mrs. Root used to smile with pleasure when Jingle came trotting up the street with Winona driving her sisters home from school.

Winona used to hitch up Jingle and drive downtown to see Joyce. It didn't matter now that Joyce lived far away. Winona could go to see her just as well as not and take her riding in the pony cart.

Winona took Lottie and Lettie riding. They went out to Page Park for a picnic.

She took Scundar and Marium riding, and little Faddoul. Her mother never forgot how much they had helped her by bringing a cake to Winona's birthday party.

She took Dennie riding. She and Dennie would plan about her Dog and Pony Show. They would teach Toodles to do tricks, Dennie said.

"And maybe Percy would ride standing up on Jingle's back," said Winona.

"I'll bet he could!" Dennie replied.

Sometimes Percy and his father and Winona and her father went riding together. They liked to go early on a summer morning before it got hot.

Betsy, Tacy, and Tib went riding in the pony cart, of course. But only once or twice. They got busy giving a show, or playing store, or having a club, or something. And of course they lived several blocks away. And Winona made friends with lots of other children, near at hand on School Street.

For a long time Winona and Betsy and Tacy and Tib didn't see each other except in school. Later on, though, they had lots of fun together.

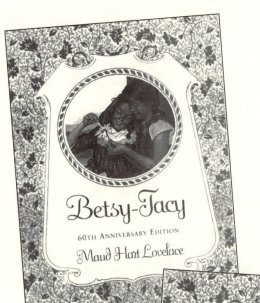

Betsy-Tacy

60TH ANNIVERSARY EDITION

Maud Hart Lovelace

A BETSY-TACY B

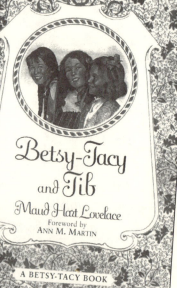

Betsy-Tacy
and Tib

Maud Hart Lovelace

Foreword by
ANN M. MARTIN

A BETSY-TACY BOOK

There are lots of children on Hill Street, but no little girls Betsy's age. So when a new family moves into the house across the street, Betsy hopes they will have a little girl she can play with. Sure enough, they do—a little girl named Tacy. And soon Betsy and Tacy become such good friends that everyone starts to think of them as one person—Betsy-Tacy.

Betsy and Tacy have lots of fun together. And one day, they come home to a wonderful surprise— a new friend named Tib!

Betsy and Tacy are best friends. Then Tib moves into the neighborhood and the three of them start to play together. The grown-ups think they will quarrel, but they don't. Sometimes they quarrel with Betsy's and Tacy's bossy big sisters, but they never quarrel among themselves.

They are not as good as they might be. They cook up awful messes in the kitchen, throw mud on each other and pretend to be beggars, and cut off each other's hair. But Betsy, Tacy, and Tib always manage to have a good time.

Betsy and Tacy
Go Over the Big Hill

Maud Hart Lovelace

Foreword by
JUDY BLUME

A BETSY-TACY B

Betsy and Tacy
Go Downtown

Maud Hart Lovelace

Foreword by
JOHANNA HURWITZ

A BETSY-TACY BOOK

Book 3: BETSY *and* TACY GO OVER *the* BIG HILL
Foreword by Judy Blume

Betsy, Tacy, and Tib can't wait to be ten—exciting things are bound to happen. And they do! The girls fall in love with the King of Spain, perform in the School Entertainment, and for the first time, go all the way over the Big Hill to Little Syria on their own. There Betsy, Tacy, and Tib make new friends and learn a thing or two. They learn that new Americans are sometimes the best Americans. And they learn that they themselves wouldn't want to be anything else.

Book 4: BETSY *and* TACY GO DOWNTOWN
Foreword by Johanna Hurwitz

Betsy, Tacy, and Tib are twelve—old enough to do lots of things . . . even go downtown on their own. They see their first horseless carriage, discover the joys of the public library, and see a real play at the Opera House. They even find themselves acting in one! Best of all, they help a lonely new friend feel at home in Deep Valley—the most wonderful place in the world to grow up.